PERCH

D0192236

This Little Tiger book belongs to:

return / renew by date shown.

can renew it at:

_____

_____

For Arthur, the bravest knight in the kingdom! With love x
~ T C

For Cora - my newest cousin (twice removed!)
~ A E

LITTLE TIGER PRESS
1 The Coda Centre, 189 Munster Road,
London SW6 6AW
www.littletiger.co.uk

First published in Great Britain 2015
This edition published 2015

Text copyright © Tracey Corderoy 2015
Illustrations copyright © Alison Edgson 2015
Tracey Corderoy and Alison Edgson have asserted their rights to be
identified as the author and illustrator of this work under the
Copyright, Designs and Patents Act, 1988

A CIP catalogue record for this book is
available from the British Library

All rights reserved • ISBN 978-1-84869-049-3

Printed in China • LTP/1400/1000/1114

2 4 6 8 10 9 7 5 3 1

I Want My Daddy!

Tracey Corderoy

Alison Edgson

LITTLE TIGER PRESS
London

Arthur was having a bad day.
His castle kept tumbling down.
   "Too wibbly," Arthur frowned.
"Too wobbly!"
   He picked up Huffity and stomped
away. "I want my daddy!" he grumbled.

"Daddy," groaned Arthur,
"my castle's gone all *wrong!*"
  "Oh dear," said Daddy. "Let's see!"
And he followed his little knight
through the garden.

"Hmmm," Daddy nodded, "this looks like a job for more than *one* knight."

"Are *you* a knight too, Daddy?" Arthur asked.

"I certainly am!" Daddy smiled. "Knights together?"

"Knights forever!" cried Arthur.

Arthur's daddy found a big pot of glue. "This," he said, "is castle *cement!*"

"Oooo!" gasped Arthur, stepping closer.

He helped Daddy to cement and paint, and make the turrets nice and straight.

"And all castles need a flag," Arthur said, popping one on the top.

"There!" he cried. "We did it! Yippee!"
"Good work!" Daddy chuckled.

While Daddy finished his own jobs, Arthur played knights with Huffity.

He marched and climbed.
He swished his sword.
Then he found a good horse and galloped off . . .

"Charge!" roared Arthur, chasing baddies from his kingdom – faster, and faster,

until ...

"Ouch," squeaked Arthur,
rubbing his leg. He took
a deep breath and cried,

"Daddy!"

"Cheer up, my big brave knight!" said Daddy, dashing over with a hug. "How about we visit your *favourite* castle?"

"The one in the park?" Arthur said. "That's Huffity's favourite castle too!"

So off they went together.

"Here we are!" said Daddy.
"Hooray!" Arthur cheered.
The castle had turrets and
ladders and a great big slide!

They marched
around it.

They climbed up . . .

and slid down. And they
talked about kings and
crowns.

PLEASE CLOSE
THE GATE

"Now let's fish for monsters in the moat!" cried Arthur. So they sat side by side, and waited, and waited . . .

Then, suddenly something tugged at Arthur's line.

"Daddy – a monster!" yelled Arthur.
"I've caught one!"

But what if it was big?

And hairy?

And scary!

"Daddy!"

"Here I am!" called Daddy. "I was just getting our snacks."

"But I've caught a monster!" Arthur cried.
Arthur wasn't scared now his daddy was here.

So they pulled, and pulled, and pulled,
until . . .

Splosh!

Out came
the monster!
"A Boot-a-saurus!" Daddy chuckled.
"A Boot-a-saurus?" giggled Arthur.
And they laughed and laughed
all the way home.

Later, tucked away in his castle in the garden, Arthur made a big sparkly crown. Every knight needed a king for his castle. And Arthur's king was to be someone very special . . .

Someone who was missing him, right now.

"Arthur?" called Daddy.

"Arthur? Where are you . . . ?"

"Surprise!"

shouted Arthur, jumping out and popping
the crown on Daddy's head.

"Hugs together?" Daddy asked.

"Hugs forever!" cheered Arthur.
And he gave his daddy the biggest hug
in the *whole* kingdom!

More romping reads for little knights!

Big and Small
Elizabeth Bennett
Jane Chapman

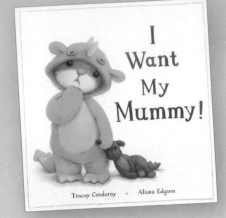

I Want My Mummy!
Tracey Corderoy • Alison Edgson

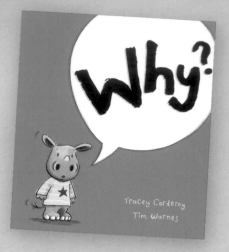

Why?
Tracey Corderoy
Tim Warnes

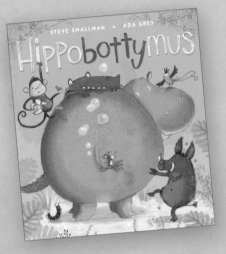

STEVE SMALLMAN • ADA GREY
Hippobottymus

Tracey Corderoy • Alison Edgson
Just One More!

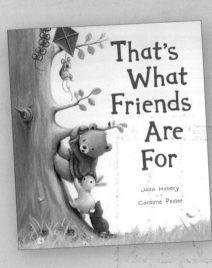

That's What Friends Are For
Julia Hubery
Caroline Pedler

For information regarding any other Little Tiger Press
titles or for our catalogue, please contact us:
Little Tiger Press, 1 The Coda Centre,
189 Munster Road, London SW6 6AW
Tel: 020 7385 6333 • Fax: 020 7385 7333
E-mail: contact@littletiger.co.uk • www.littletiger.co.uk